Rob me Blindly

FLIPPED FAIRYTALES

HARLOWE SAVAGE

This is for every Sapphic reader who's ever dreamed about disappearing into the woods to be cottagecore lesbians. 🩶

Chapter One

"It's a really good thing that we picked you up." The man leered at Marian from his seat across the carriage. "These parts are riddled with bandits just looking to take advantage of a pretty little thing like you."

Marian forced her lips into a smile, unable to focus on anything other than the piece of gristle, stuck grotesquely between the man's protruding teeth. It moved when he spoke, but not enough to dislodge itself, only enough to turn Marian's stomach.

"Yes. When my horse spooked and ran away, I didn't know what I was going to do." Marian replied, keeping her hands folded neatly in her lap. She tilted her head slightly, leaning into the damsel-in-distress act. "I was so fortunate that you found me and offered me a ride."

The man pursed his lips, nodding sagely. Marian watched as the corners of his mouth fought the urge to turn up in an unsettling grin and did her best not to grimace.

The man's wife shifted uncomfortably in her seat as she sighed heavily. Her spindly form, resembling a willow tree, was dwarfed by the man's rotund frame that took up more than half the bench. Quite the pair to behold, the couple couldn't have been more than lower level nobles, but were dressed as though they were none other than the King and Queen attending their own coronations.

The man was stuffed into an obscenely extravagant doublet like a sausage packed into a casing, his neck spilling out over the high collar, smothering the lace trim. Then the woman, though smaller, was no less indulgent and expressed her taste for the decadent through her gown, made of wool and embroidered with fine silks.

"We are lucky that we weren't attacked when stopping for her." The woman shot a venomous glare at the man. "There's a reason merchants warn you not to stop in these woods, Sherwood forest is the territory of the Merry Men."

"Fucking bunch of jagoffs they are, calling themselves the Merry Men, all while robbing good, hardworking nobles blind." The man's lip turned up in a sneer as he jostled the carriage with the sheer weight of his movement as he adjusted in his seat, crossing his arms.

Good, hardworking nobles - Marian had to hold back a scoff, she'd never heard of such a thing.

"Yes, well." Marian turned her head to look out the window at the passing Aspen and Birch trees. The familiar sound of a wood pigeon call inspired a nigh undetectable grin before she turned back to the pair.

"I am very fortunate, indeed, that you rescued me. I would have hated to have a run in with people like that."

The man cleared his throat, puffing his chest.

"Don't worry, I'm sure you'll find a way to thank me properly when we arrive at the next town."

Marian felt the corner of her mouth twitch, pulling down

slightly at the thought of what the man was implying, but quickly shook it off. If looks could kill, Marian would have been dead ten times over by the pointed glare she was receiving from the noblewoman.

Too many marriages were like this these days, women holding the victims of their husbands' foul lust accountable for the men's terrible actions. However misdirected, Marian tried not to hold it against her - surely, she was the true victim here, forced to spend every day attending to the every need of this gluttonous cretin.

"I'm sure I will." Marian smiled despite the woman's scowl.

The woman opened her mouth to speak, but before she could get out whatever protest she surely had primed, the carriage ground to a screeching halt. Marian dug her heels into the floor, gripping the wall in an effort to remain seated and not thrown into the laps of the unhappy couple in front of her.

"What in the devil?" The man cried, bracing himself on the carriage door. "Hendrix, son, are you touched? We shouldn't be stopping here!"

There was the sound of horses settling and in the brief respite

"What?" The wife sneered, turning her attention back to the man while fixing her hair and dress. "No beautiful damsel in distress to pick up this time?"

The man shot his wife a punishing look before turning in his seat and banging on the front wall of the carriage. "Hendrix! What the fuck are you doing up there?"

"There's a downed tree, sir." The young carriage driver called from outside, his voice muffled by the wall. "I can try to go around it but - arghhh!"

Marian perked up as the carriage shifted with a thud.

"Hendrix? Hendrix!" The nobleman called out, alarmed as the young driver's voice was cut off, mid response.

"Douglas, what's going on?" The woman clutched her breast, irritation all but forgotten looking quickly back and forth, as if anticipating an attack from all sides. The pair paused for a moment, listening for their driver, but were met only by silence and the tittering sounds of the forest.

"Stay here." The nobleman huffed in exertion as he stepped out of the carriage, the coach groaning with the movement, finally springing up as he stepped out. One hand on the hilt of his sword, he shuffled out of sight.

Marian held her breath as she listened to the sound of the man's footsteps, making their way around to the front when she heard the telltale sound of a sword being drawn.

"Who are you? And what do you want with my- ugh..."

The sound of the man's paunchy body hitting the dirt road was shortly followed by a sharp whistle and a few more wood pigeon calls echoing through the trees. The noblewoman stared across the coach, panic in her eyes as another set of footsteps approached the door. When it finally swung open, she gasped at the hooded visage that stood before them.

The hooded figure took one cursory glance around the carriage before throwing the cape back, revealing a head of gorgeous, red hair. Turning her attention to Marian, she grinned widely, offering a hand.

Finally allowing herself to relax, Marian allowed the tension to drain from her posture, shifting forward. A smile crept back to her face as she reached out, placing her hand in the ranger's.

"Robin, what took you so long?"

Robin shook her head, the smile never leaving her face as

she helped Marian out of the carriage - much to the shock of the noblewoman, still seated and frozen in fear.

"Apologies, my love." Robin wrapped her hands around Marian's waist, lifting her and gently placing her onto solid ground. "Joanna seemed to misplace the felling axe, so we got a little bit of a late start this morning."

"Goodness." Marian teased, interlacing her fingers with Robin's. "What would you have done if they'd actually managed to get me to the next town? I'm confident that Douglas over there was dead set on ravaging me in the nearest inn he could find."

Robin chuckled, leading Marian to the front of the carriage. "You know I would have never allowed that to happen. I would simply have had to storm the town and rescue you, I suppose, no matter how inconvenient."

The pair moved past Hendrix and Douglas, gagged and tied to a tree off the side of the road. The captives were watching Marian and Robin with striking emotions that ranged from shock on the part of the driver to the blind fury of the nobleman.

"Oh, don't lie." Marian tucked a strand of hair behind her ear with her free hand. "You love to storm towns and break rules - rescuing me would have been the cherry on top."

Robin laughed, throwing her head back, the joyous sound infectious to everyone who heard it. Marian's gaze softened as she appreciated the way the filtered sunlight danced in Robin's hair. Releasing the other woman's hand, Marian raised her palms to cup Robin's face, bringing their lips together in a gentle kiss. Robin hummed, her arms winding around Marian's waist and pulling her close.

Marian opened her lips, throwing her arms around Robin's

neck and kissing her lover more deeply. She meant to continue but paused when someone cleared their throat.

"There will be plenty of time for that later." The someone continued.

Marian pulled back, remaining happily in Robin's arms as she looked over her shoulder to see Willa leaning against the carriage, the noblewoman standing subdued next to her.

Robin chuckled, tightening her arms around Marian's waist. "But Willa, what will we do while you empty the chests of valuables?"

Willa scoffed, gesturing for the noblewoman to sit as she shoved her hands in her pockets and approached. "Help us. This was your raid, pardon me for assuming that you were going to, I don't know, raid?"

Marian smiled at the teasing words, turning back to Robin. "You know, my love. She is right. You wouldn't be a very good thief if you didn't steal anything."

Robin placed a hand to her chest in faux offense. "I resent that. I've stolen plenty of things, forgive me if I simply want to give my Merry Men the opportunity to show off."

Willa snorted, pointing an accusatory finger at Robin's chest. "Sure, sure. Keep talking and we'll have you carrying all the loot back to the hideout singlehandedly."

Robin grinned at the empty threat before throwing her hands up in surrender. "Fine, fine. I'm going."

Marian watched as Robin ducked behind the carriage with a wink before wandering over and leaning up against the cabin, arms crossed. When within the suffocating confines of the city, she never allowed herself to stand with anything less than the perfect posture. However, here, among friends, she granted herself this small luxury.

"You set us up!" The noblewoman huffed from her seat on a nearby log. "I knew we never should have stopped for you."

Marian turned around to face her with a shrug. "Perhaps. Or maybe, you were just unlucky."

The woman frowned, her lips puckering like she'd sucked down lemon juice. Gaze wandering from the wife, Marian pushed off the carriage and placed a hand, gently on the hindquarters of the dapple Thoroughbred attached to the left harness.

"You know how to tell the difference between old money and new money?" Marian paused, feeling the twitching muscles of the horse under her fingers. "Lots of people think it's the clothing or the type of fringe adorning the cabin of their carriage, but truthfully it's none of those things."

Marian smiled, tilting her head back towards the noblewoman.

"Dapple Thoroughbreds are rare, and expensive to acquire." Ignoring the confusion that overtook the woman's face, Marian continued, dragging her hand up the side of the animal as she made her way to its front, holding its face in her hands.

"Anyone who's ever shopped for a horse would know that. But, people who've been around enough generational wealth know that the best choice for a horse-drawn carriage is an Arabian."

Glancing back past the dapple, Marian flashed a smile at the woman who was now staring openly, mouth agape, like a fish.

"Thoroughbreds are wonderful horses, but their strengths are primarily in speed for short distances, while Arabians are more built for endurance - like pulling a carriage from city to city. Furthermore, Arabians tend to have stronger hooves and don't require shoes like Thoroughbreds do, again, much more suited to long distances on rough country roads.

Anyway, it's too risky to rob anyone with old money since they likely have a connection to some very important people. But new money - well, the second I saw your pair of dapples making their way up the road, I knew you'd be an easy mark - so I just signaled to the Merry Men waiting in the woods and stepped out to be picked up.

"But don't worry." Marian continued, sitting into her hip and crossing her arms. "We won't take any of your clothes, rations, or horses. Once we leave you'll be free to untie your driver and husband and be on your way. The Merry Men aren't killers, we just simply believe in a... different sort of wealth distribution system."

The woman clicked her teeth, but said nothing more, instead opting to resume scowling at her husband, likely reigniting her original grievance that they should have never picked up a strange girl in the woods in the first place. Marian assumed that while the man would likely never hear the end of it, there clearly wasn't any love lost between the pair and Marian got the feeling that it probably wouldn't be the first, nor the only thing she nagged him about.

"Alright, that should be everything." Willa's voice called. "Now we just need to help Johanna's team finish cutting up the log and moving it off the road and we'll be on our way."

With only a few moments' warning to Robin's approach from behind, Marian hummed in acknowledgement as Robin wrapped her arms around her waist once again, placing her chin on Marian's shoulder like a cat.

"There's one thing I don't understand." Marian turned her

head to the tree where their hostages were tied up. The young carriage driver managed to get free of his gag and was watching the group with curious eyes. "Why go by the Merry Men, you're all..."

"Women?" Robin finished and Marian could hear the grin in her voice. The boy nodded, confusion clouding his expression.

"Well, that's simple." Robin released her lover and walked around to stand next to her, hands on her hips. "Because it's funny."

"Nobody ever expects the feared Merry Men to be a bunch of ladies." Willa piped up, dusting her hands off on her pants. "So people either don't believe us or resolve to keep quiet because their pride can't handle the thought of being jumped by a gaggle of dames."

"I can't read minds," Robin shrugged, walking casually over to where Douglas was tied up. "But, if I were a betting woman-"

"Which you are." Joanna called with a grunt as she and the other Merry Men pushed the remaining pieces out of the road.

Robin smiled wildly, leaning forward to make eye contact with the nobleman, keeping her hands in her pockets.

"Which I am. I would bet that Douglas here will fall into the latter of the two categories."

"What makes you say that?" The boy asked, withering back at the sharp look Douglas threw his way as he spoke up.

"Well." Robin continued. "I imagine that he's going to catch enough shit about this for a lifetime from the missus here, so I just find it hard to believe that he would open himself up to further opportunity for ridicule by telling his betters. Right, Douglas?"

Douglas avoided her gaze as his face turned bright red with anger, but to Marian's surprise, as Robin stood back up and began to walk away, he didn't even try to say anything at all.

Chapter Two

It would have been too much of a hassle to bring an extra horse for Marian but she really didn't mind. One less horse meant that she got to share with Robin and that was never something she would complain about. With Marian cozied up in front of Robin on their horse, the pair made their way down the dirt road and away from the scene of the crime, Johanna following close behind. The rest of the Merry Men had split off in their different directions and begun making their way to camp through their various decoy routes. It was unlikely that Douglas and his wife were a royal set-up in an effort to track down the band of thieves but after every single job they still split up this way, as a precaution, to confuse anyone potentially tailing them.

The gentle rocking of the horse as it walked almost lulled Marian into complete relaxation until she caught a glimpse of which direction they were heading.

"Isn't this the way to town?" Marian turned in her seat.

Robin grinned and adjusted her grip on the reins. "Very observant, my dear."

Marian pouted. "But I'm not ready to go back yet."

"Who said anything about going back?" Johanna piped up from behind.

Robin pulled Marian in closer until she was pressed up against her warm chest, practically spooning. "Ester needs Johanna to relieve her at the convent - so I figured that we could take the scenic road. What do you think about that?"

Marian nodded, much happier after being set straight.

Each of the Merry Men had a job in the city that allowed them to be perfectly primed for distribution in one capacity or another; traveling merchants, women of the cloth, people who wouldn't raise alarms if they went missing for a couple of weeks.

The Friar, in charge of running the dilapidated church on the outskirts of town, frequently covered for the rotation of "sisters" coming and going from the woods. Marian didn't know very much about the Friar, but she knew that Robin trusted him and that was enough for her.

It wasn't odd for a church to be a source of relief for the residents of poorer neighborhoods, so in that way, it was the perfect cover. Furthermore the Friar was always careful to ration the wealth the Merry Men redistributed into his care so as to not attract too much attention.

The Crown was convinced that the group of thieves living in Sherwood Forest was a group of ex-military men who had become jaded after their years in service. Marian remembered a conversation stating as much between the Prince and his father several months ago. As a result, nobody was looking for the odd woman handing out extra food and coin at the church or next to the neighborhood community center. The Merry Men had been operating this way for years, but Marian still felt better knowing that their movements remained unnoticed as a result of patriarchal ego.

Incognito was exactly the way Robin liked to keep things - in all the years Marian had known her, Robin never sought fame or recognition for the things that she did, only doing what she thought was right. It was one of the many things Marian loved about her.

Before she started running with Robin's crew, Marian would sometimes hide out on the outskirts of town to get away from it all - her many years of dodging the guard shifts was how she knew that it was very unlikely that they'd be seen at this time of day. As "serious" as the Sheriff was about keeping crime to a minimum, he certainly shirked on his duties in regards to patrolling the less fortunate areas of the town, unless it was tax collection day, that is.

Pretty soon, the expansive forest fell away to rolling oceans of wheat and crops. The church wasn't so much within the actual limits of the town as it hovered at the edge, peppered in amongst the barns and farmhouses.

Approaching the church, Marian relaxed into the saddle as the cobbled walls of the rectory came into focus - despite not spending very much time there, the church had become some-what of a haven for Marian. Knowing that at least one of the Merry Men was stationed there all times helped her rest on the nights that she tossed and turned in her palace room. The warm candlelight of the church always shone in the distance outside her window and soothed her when she needed it.

Robin slowed their horse to a stop at the fence and dismounted, reaching up to help Marian.

"You're early this week." The Friar's jovial voice rang through the air as he made his way outside, a cross bouncing against his brown robe with each step down the stairs.

"We happened to get extra lucky." Robin grinned, interlacing her hand with Marian's and walking over to greet the older man. "We weren't going to be able to store everything until Thursday so Johanna and I figured we would take a bit of a detour before heading back to camp."

The Friar smiled, peering over his round glasses at the trio when he laid eyes on Marian and his grin vanished. He peered conspiratorially over his shoulder before hurrying the three of them off the church lawn and towards the barn.

"Marian, my dear. You shouldn't be here right now." The Friar's voice turned hushed as he shooed them around the corner to the side of the church.

Robin dropped Marian's hand. "Why? What's going on?"

"The Sheriff is here. He cannot see the two of you, lest he start putting the pieces together."

Marian's blood ran cold, as she chanced a peek through the stained glass - doing her best to watch for motion inside the church.

Robin nodded curtly. "We'll go around to the back, drop the gold off in the coffers box. Marian, it might be best for you to try and meet us back at camp."

Marian frowned but nodded, watching Robin and Johanna move silently, but quickly in the opposite direction before following the Friar back around to the front. They had almost made it to the horses when the sickening voice of Sheriff Philip Mark boomed from the front door.

"Marian."

Marian flinched, she couldn't help it. Everything about the Sheriff made her skin crawl, from his demeanor and the way he carried himself down to his smell, his lack of daily bathing drowned in cheap cologne. She couldn't bring herself to turn around, instead clutching at the Friar's hand like a lifeline.

"The Prince was looking for you this morning."

Patting Marian gently on the top of her hand, the Friar turned them both around, lending Marian the strength she needed to finally move.

"Ah yes, that was my fault, you see. Marian came down this morning to help me with some of the chores around the rectory. She meant to be back by lunch but I insisted that she stay so I could thank her."

Marian let her gaze drift up from the dirt where it had landed and onto the self-satisfied grin of the Sheriff, turning her stomach.

"Yes." Marian nodded, trying her best to remember her manners. "Please let the Prince know that I will be back this evening."

The Sheriff's lip curled up as he shoved his hands into his pockets. "I think it's probably best if you let me take you back. He was *very* worried after all."

Marian clenched her jaw, imagining being alone in the carriage with him set off every fight or flight response she'd ever developed over the years. She couldn't even stand looking the man in the eye, God forbid she would be trapped in an enclosed space with him for any period of time. Technically, she was under the protection of the Prince, but there was no telling what he would and wouldn't try if there were no witnesses.

For a horrible moment, there was silence, only the sound of

the birds chirping and the wind in the trees, but then a familiar voice called from the front door.

"Lady Marian, Friar! Oh, please excuse me Sheriff." Marian's gaze snapped to the space behind where the Sheriff had emerged, letting out a breath of relief at the image of Johanna, no, Sister Johannas, now in a nun's habit, beckoning them inside.

"What is it, Sister?" Marian saw the subtle lowering of the Friar's shoulders as he gratefully accepted the out turning his full attention to the door.

"I'm terribly sorry, but I need the Lady Marian's help with a couple of things in the kitchen. Sister Helen is feeling under the weather and there is no way we will be able to prepare the Soup Kitchen for this evening without her."

Johanna clasped her hands in front of her, pausing for a moment in faux thought before speaking up again. "Unless of course, you would like to help, Sir?"

Marian bit the inside of her cheek as to not grin at the disgusted look that crossed the Sheriff's face at the prospect of participating in "women's work".

"No. That's quite alright." The Sheriff acquiesced unhappily. "I'll just make sure to let the Prince know to expect you this evening."

Marian nodded and hurried up the stairs and into the rectory, all the time trying not to shudder at the feeling of the Sheriff's eyes on her back. Once she got to the kitchen, Marian busied herself with the dishes. She couldn't truly focus on her task while the Sheriff was still so nearby, the ghost of his gaze crawling over her skin like cockroaches. So instead, she did her very best to look busy, scrubbing away absentmindedly at the same pot until she was absolutely sure that the Sheriff had gone, watching him leave through the window.

Pursing her lips, she let the pot fall into the soapy water, as the carriage took off towards the palace. Frustrated, she grabbed the towel hanging on a hook on the wall and dried her hands, only keeping it together as she heard Robin approaching from behind once again.

"He's gone." Robin snaked her arms around Marian's waist, but before she could pull her in, Marian turned around in her hold, burying her face in Robin's neck.

"I know." Marian's voice was muffled by the fabric of Robin's shirt and her hair, giving Marian a safe place to hide.

"You alright?" Robin's fingers trailed up and down Marian's spine as Marian felt the last of the tension leave her body.

"I'm fine." Marian pulled back slightly, still wrapped in Robin's embrace. "His seeing me is just going to complicate things. I didn't tell anyone I was leaving this morning, so inevitably the Prince is going to get suspicious."

"I know." Robin replied softly, cupping Marian's cheek. "Do you want to go back now?"

Marian shook her head with a sigh. "When I do go back, Prince John likely isn't going to let me out of his sight for a while. So, I might as well stay out as long as I can - get the most out it before I'm confined to my room as punishment."

Robin nodded, her eyes gentle with understanding. "Well, in that case, we should head back to camp just in case the Prince decides to send someone here to pick you up. Can't make it *too* easy for them, now can we?"

Marian laughed, appreciative of the way Robin was able to turn her mood around regardless of the situation. Despite only knowing her for a small percentage of her life, Robin knew

Marian better than anyone else ever could. Robin wasn't just her lover, she was... everything to her.

Robin slid her hands down the sides of Marian's arms and took her hands before tilting her head in the direction of the stables.

Marian knew that she couldn't run forever, but at least for the rest of the day, she wanted to pretend that she could.

Chapter Three

The ride back to camp was short and uneventful; they weren't going directly from a robbery so they didn't need to take extremely evasive measures. Once they arrived, Robin hopped down off their horse, helping Marian out of the saddle as well before turning and greeting Alana. Located in a blind spot directly between two watch towers, the Merry Men's camp was well lived in, but still as temporary as it could be so the group could be ready to leave at a moment's notice.

Marian held tight to Robin's hand as the thief discussed final numbers with their treasurer. Every single coin that the Merry Men pinched, save for the haul that was brought directly to the Friar, went into a tent set up on top of a wagon at the edge of camp to be distributed at a later date. Robin was very strict about living off the land as much as they could, only taking gold for supplies that could not be hunted or foraged - both in an effort to avoid detection and as part of the principles she lived by.

Once the conversation turned further from business and

back towards lighter topics, Marian decided that she'd waited long enough for some quality time with Robin. Tugging gently on Robin's hand was enough for the other woman to say a quick goodbye and allow Marian to lead her towards Robin's tent. With one more look around to ensure that nobody was coming to interrupt them, Marian loosed the door tie-backs and slipped inside as the fabric fell down over the entrance.

The moment the tent flaps closed behind them, Robin reached out, burying her fingers in Marian's tousled hair and bringing their lips together. Marian smiled into the kiss, it had been too long since she'd been able to sneak out and the long nights of solitude had her patience at its wits end.

Underneath the leather vest and linen shirt, Robin was solid muscle from her years of roughing it in the woods.

Marian loved how solid she felt next to her own soft, pampered body and wasted no time slipping her hands up under Robin's top, tracing the quivering ab muscles with a reverence that she saved only for her lover.

With a gasp, Robin removed her hands from Marian's hair, and gripped the backs of her thighs, lifting her up onto the table in the middle of the tent. Marian spread her legs, allowing Robin to step between them as she dragged her hands up Marian's back from her thighs and back into her hair, taking every opportunity she could to touch each curve and sensitive spot she encountered on the way.

Marian opened her mouth, pressing forward into Robin's kisses as she wrapped her legs around her lover's waist. She could already feel herself getting wet, Robin's smell, the feel of her body against her own - it had been so long and her body craved Robin like it craved water. Desperately, Marian moved her hands to Robin's pants, fumbling with the laces at the front. She wanted her hands on her, now.

Robin gasped, hips moving forward into her touch as she pulled at Marian's skirts, until they were out of the way, bunched up around her hips. Robin kissed a trail down Marian's jaw and neck, one hand gripping Marian's hair and the other traveling forward, between her legs.

When Marian finally got Robin's pants undone, she slipped her hand inside to find Robin already wet, grinding forward desperate for any sort of friction. Robin's hips stuttered as Marian's fingers passed further down, over her clit and between her lips. As much as she wanted to focus on pleasuring her lover, Robin's hand had also found its way between her own legs and as her thumb began stroking her, it was all she could do to slip her fingers inside and let Robin ride her hand as she gave way to the pleasure.

The pair puffed and panted, their lips finding each other once more, deepening their kisses until they were simply tongues and wet gasps.

"Robin..." Marian murmured, feeling her core heating up. Rolling her hips forward into Robin's touch, she opened her mouth, a plea already forming on her lips, but stopped at the sound of another voice outside.

"Robin." Willa called from immediately outside the tent.

Robin huffed, hips stilling for a moment as the pair stopped, breaths still intermingling. Marian could feel Robin rock her hips slightly as she tried to remain level. "Now is really not a good time, WIlla."

Marian smiled, nipping at Robin's jaw and ear - taking the initiative to start moving her hand once more, fucking Robin with her fingers. Robin hummed, eyes drifting shut as she braced herself against the table.

"That's why I didn't come in, but we just got word that Prince John sent out a search party for Marian. We need to get her back to the palace before they start a search in this part of the woods."

Robin whimpered, clenching against Marian's fingers and for a moment she was silent - like she was weighing the risks of getting found with finishing what they'd started - but eventually sighed and removed Marian's hand from her pants, pressing one final kiss to her lips.

"Fuck." She murmured under her breath before stepping back and calling out to Willa. "Fine, fine. I'll deliver her back now. Go ready the horse."

Marian sighed. As much as she desperately wanted to continue, Willa was right. The only reason the guards hadn't found the Merry Men's camp yet was due to its strategically placed location between two guard towers. If they started a grid search, there was no doubt that they'd be discovered.

"Well, I suppose we should get going." Marian pursed her lips, pushing her skirt back down. Robin unhappily laced her pants and pushed her hair out of her face - her expression looking quite literally, pained.

Marian hopped down from the table and walked over to Robin, taking her face gently in her hands.

"One of these days we will be able to have some time just to ourselves, where we won't be interrupted."

"Mmm." Robin took Marian's hand and pulled it up to her lips, pressing a kiss to her knuckles. "And when will that be?" Marian burned as Robin's tongue darted out, briefly tasting the fingers that had just been inside of her.

Marian took a shuddering breath, leaning forward and touching their foreheads together, trying desperately to cool down.

"When my presence doesn't put you and the Merry Men in danger." Marian smiled softly. "One of these days he will grow weary of my rejections and seek out another potential wife."

"And if he doesn't?" Robin played mindlessly with Marian's fingers.

"Then we will simply have to run away." Marian assured her. "But let's not cross that bridge yet - when I get to leave the palace I want it to be as a free woman. As much as you love the woods, I know that you want to settle down in a nice little cottage where I can plant a garden and we can live off the land. We can't really do that if I'm being hunted."

Robin sighed and pulled Marian into a tight hug, the pair finally equalizing and backing down from the lust filled cliff. "I know. To be fair though, I'm also being hunted. We could be on the run together - it would be very romantic."

Marian chuckled. "Yes, but Prince John doesn't know what you look like. Once you give up the moniker 'Robin Hood of Sherwood Forest', nobody will ever be the wiser."

"I know." Robin smiled back. "I suppose we really should get going, before my desire for you overcomes my common sense."

Marian laughed under her breath and followed Robin outside. Willa, who at least had the decency to look a bit sheepish for interrupting their alone time, stood a few feet away, reins in hand. And as much as Marian wished she could disappear for a while longer, she understood. With Marian back at the palace, there would be no reason for Prince John to continue his search and as much as she wanted to stay she wouldn't be the reason Robin and the Merry Men got caught.

"We'll see you around, alright?" The corners of Willa's mouth turned up in a grin as she addressed Marian, handing the reins over to Robin.

"Course. Couldn't get rid of me if you tried." Marian joked back, clearing the air of any remaining awkwardness.

Robin mounted first, throwing her leg over the saddle and settling in before leaning over to the side. Marian hopped in time with Robin's hands gripping her waist and Robin pulled her up into the saddle alongside her before grabbing the reins again, trapping Marian against her chest.

"I'll be back tonight." Robin announced. "Don't wait up, alright?"

Willa nodded and the pair took off on horseback. The journey was slow in the beginning as the backwoods were treacherous terrain, especially on horseback - but they couldn't risk going directly to the road from the camp. So, as the horse shifted side to side, carefully stepping over roots and logs, Marian did her best to stay still, leaning into Robin.

However, once they crossed the boundary from no-man's land into the patrol area of the southern guard tower, Robin navigated them up onto the road, heading into town.

Throwing her hood up over her face, Robin relaxed into Marian as the horse did a majority of the work on the easy road.

"So." Robin began, waving idly to a passing merchant cart. "Tell me more about this cottage you were talking about."

Marian smiled and began to describe the home she always imagined she and Robin would make together as they made their way to the gates.

Nottingham was a lovely, little town right on the outskirts

of the forest with a river running through the town square. The red brick buildings and peaked, shingled roofs teased their way just over the treeline if one cared to look and off in the distance, the iron cross atop the town church stood against the sky like a beacon of salvation.

It would be considered a modest town if not for Nottingham Palace in the very center. Its tall walls and vibrant flags a constant reminder to the villagers and all surrounding residents whom their taxes went to every month.

Marian despised living in the palace, but she'd been placed there as a ward of the King when she was quite young. Her plan had always been to leave once she turned 18, but once the Prince began taking an interest in her, that possibility became less and less of a potential reality every day.

The first time she ran away, she'd barely made it past the gates before the King's guards were trotting up next to her on their horses. As time passed, she got smarter, climbing out her window instead of walking out the front door, scaling the wall and dropping down into a pile of hay instead of chancing the gates. However, unfortunately for her, the more she ran, the more adamant the Prince became about hunting her down. She had almost given up entirely by her 20th birthday when she met Robin.

Robin, who was posing as a traveling merchant, caught her slipping into a stable to avoid guards and Marian had been immediately enamoured.

This was what she'd been missing, the soft touch of another woman, with her curves and full lips. Once they'd lain together just one time, Marian knew that she would never be able to bear the Prince's children. The thought of any man touching her in the way that Robin did made her sick to her stomach and she knew that she needed to discourage the Prince's advances more directly.

Despite her resolution, however, it had been three years since that day and Marian was no closer to freedom than she'd been the day the King dropped her off at the palace door.

Chapter Four

The next morning was a sordid affair, she'd already gotten quite the earful from Prince John the night before when she'd strolled down from her room as if nothing had happened, wrapped in one of her many robes. She tried insisting that she'd come directly back after her time at the church, but the Prince wasn't buying it. Over the years, he'd found all her hiding places, exposed all the corners of the palace where she'd once felt safe, and one of the reasons she took off now was simply to escape his ever-present eye.

However, despite her hopes that the Prince would just let it go, it seemed that the night before had only been the beginning and that she was, unfortunately, in for a very difficult day.

The morning began with Marian waking up to the light sound of her handmaiden, Ella, knocking on the door.

"Come in." Marian yawned, sitting up in her bed and rubbing her eyes. Ella slipped in, closing the door behind her to preserve her lady's modesty.

"I'm terribly sorry for waking you up so early, my Lady, but the Prince insisted that I invite you down to breakfast."

Marian paused, looking over at Ella to ensure that she'd

heard her correctly. The Prince rarely woke up early enough to have breakfast with her, let alone beat her to the dining room; so waking up to an invitation like this one did not bode well.

After she'd dressed and sent Ella off to do her daily chores, she quickly made her way down to the dining hall and sure enough, as she entered, there he was, sitting at the head of the table.

Marian took her seat and graciously accepted the wine being served, deciding that she might need it. And sure enough, no sooner than she had swallowed her first mouthful, did the Prince begin to speak.

"I don't know why you continue to insist on lying to me." John grumbled, knife scratching against his porcelain dish as he cut the meat on his plate.

"I'm sure I don't know what you mean, Sire." Marian responded, popping a piece of bread into her mouth.

Prince John's fist came down on the table with a thud that startled Marian, snapping her gaze up to meet her companion's across the table. The Prince was not a violent man, and as a result, Marian rarely experienced any of his outbursts directly, so it caught her by surprise, stunning her into momentary silence.

"You *weren't* at the palace yesterday. You were out in the woods again, cavorting with thieves and criminals."

Prince John frowned, his brows furrowing and deepening the lines on his face. Despite being nearly 30, his hair was unruly, like it had always been as a child and the crown he wore on his head was several sizes too large, slipping down over his ears when he moved around too much. He'd always sworn that he was going to grow into it, but after one poorly timed comment from the jewel-smith a few years ago, it became an unspoken rule among the residents of the palace never to point it out.

Taking a deep breath, Marian regained her composure, pushing a grape around her plate.

"I don't know why you keep insisting that." Marian's lips pulled down into a scowl. "What if I was simply taking a walk around the palace grounds? Wouldn't you feel foolish then?"

John huffed, letting his silverware clatter to the table.

"We need to have a serious conversation and since you insist on dodging my attempts to have it in private, I suppose it needs to happen right now."

Marian's gaze flicked back and forth to each side of the room where guards were posted at all potential exits. There was no escaping now, the conversation she'd known was coming for some time was here and there was quite literally nothing she could do to avoid it save slitting her own wrists and bleeding out on the palace floor.

"I know that you haven't missed the signs of my courting."

Marian tensed up, gripping the fork in her hand tightly, either to ground herself or to attack, she didn't know.

"I surely don't know what-"

"Yes, you do." Prince John interrupted calmly. "Marian, I've known you for years. You are many things but an idiot is not one of them."

Marian closed her eyes and took a shuddering breath. "Yes, Sire."

Prince John shifted in his seat. "I don't know why you've been so insistent on ignoring them - you and I both know that this is a smart match. We've known each other for years and as my father's third son, he's in no hurry to marry me off to a princess or noblewoman from another kingdom. He does, however, expect me to marry and as his ward, I'm sure you know that he expects that of you as well."

Marian pursed her lips and fixed her gaze upon the man she'd known for so long.

"My Lord, I have no interest in staying in Nottingham for the rest of my life. I had hoped that if I resisted your advances long enough, you would lose interest and redirect your affections to someone far more deserving of them. However, I now see that you are far too determined for that - so I'm afraid that I must decline more directly and inform you that I plan to leave the palace within the fortnight."

Marian pulled her hands into her lap to prevent anyone from seeing their trembling and waited. The Prince's face was unreadable as he watched her for a moment, perhaps expecting her to continue. Then, when she did not, he sighed and leaned to the side of his chair, folding his hands in front of him.

"Where would you even go?" Marian recoiled from the words as though she'd been struck. "You have no skills translatable outside of nobility - frankly, you owe me your life. Well, me and my father. Had you not been dropped here when you were, you would have likely been cast out onto the street, destined to freeze to death during one of Nottingham's long winters."

Marian felt her breath stick in her throat.

"Surely you don't think that he allowed you to live here out of the goodness of his heart." Prince John continued. "You were always meant to be my bride, that's why you were schooled and trained in the ways of the noble lady. Even *if* I were willing to part with you, which I am not, my father would simply never allow it."

Marian felt her mouth go dry at the confession. Of course, she'd considered the possibility that the Prince would be

unwilling to let her go, however, she truly hadn't ever considered the opinion of the King. Whether that was out of foolish-
ness or simply a misguided attempt to give herself hope was
unclear; but now that it was out on the table, all Marian could
do was sit in silence.

"Come now, Marian." Prince John shook his head and
began again with a softer tone. "It really won't be as bad as all
that. Your life can remain effectively the same, should you
choose. We would just need to have a public wedding, produce
a few children and then get on with our lives."

Marian's stomach turned. .

"You were always going to be married off to someone or
another, I don't see why it being me feels like the end of the
world."

You were always going to be married off.

Marian's breath came faster as she tried to keep herself
under control. Honestly, she hadn't thought about what would
have happened to her if the Prince had insisted upon another
match. Her thoughts immediately spiralled back to Douglas in
the carriage, with his gluttonously overfed body and crooked
teeth as he'd smiled at her predatorily when he'd thought he was
going to have his way with her.

She'd never considered the possibility that the Prince, well
within his rights to do so, could have married her off to a
random nobleman at any point.

"I see." Marian choked out, wringing her hands in her lap.
"Well, if I truly have no say in the matter, I don't see why this
conversation needed to happen at all."

The Prince sighed, pursing his lips and sitting further back
in his chair.

"Marian." John looked up at her, hands folded in his lap.

"When have I ever sprung something on you without discussing it first? You seem to forget that we are meant to be dealing with this together."

Marian was being unfair, she knew that, but if Prince John truly thought they were in the same position, he was delusional. Sure, his father was putting pressure on him to marry, but he had more of a choice in the matter than she ever would and regardless of any good intentions he had, he was still going to force her hand.

Marian cleared her throat and stood, lips trembling - the guards shifted in their posts but Prince John waved a hand, signaling them to settle again.

"I understand that you need time to process - I won't bother you for the rest of the day, but please come to dinner tomorrow prepared to discuss this matter."

Marian nodded numbly, pushing her chair back and making her way out of the dining room. The halls of the palace blurred together as Marian wandered back to her quarters - whether by orders or simply coincidence, nobody bothered to stop her.

Once the door was shut behind her, Marian shoved a chair up against it and sat heavily on the ground next to her bed. Her lip trembled as she fought back tears - she wouldn't cry, no, she'd always known that this might be a potential outcome and she wouldn't give him the satisfaction. Not that she thought he'd take satisfaction in making her cry... that was part of what was so difficult about the whole situation.

They'd grown up together and Marian always thought... no, hoped that he would care more about her wants and desires. But today's conversation just reminded her of the harsh truth of her situation.

She wanted to scream, cry, fight - anything, but above all else, she wanted to see Robin. So despite the fact that she'd only seen her yesterday and it was dangerous for the Merry Men to visit her in the palace, she walked over to her bedside table and picked up the candle. Reaching into her drawer, she pulled out a box of matches and struck one, lighting the candle before taking the chamberstick by the handle.

Marian walked over to the window and placed the candle down on the windowsill. She wasn't sure if Robin would be able to see it during the daytime, but she had plenty of candles and nothing but time.

Marian had long since fallen asleep, exhausted from her attempts to hold back her tears and woke very suddenly to a rap on her door. Sprawled out on her comforter, Marian did not move to get up, instead looking back over at the windowsill where her third candle was about to go out. It was dark outside now and the warmth of the flame fluttered in the glass pane of the window.

Determined to not be bothered, Marian allowed her eyes to drift shut once again, willing herself back to sleep. However, whoever was outside her door seemed undeterred from her lack of response and knocked yet again.

"Go away." Marian huffed, turning over onto her side. "Prince John said I'd be left alone until tomorrow." In response, the hallway was quiet and for a moment Marian thought that she'd succeeded in frightening away the interloper, but then a familiar voice reached her ears.

"I can leave if you want, but I was under the impression that you called for me."

Marian sat up straight at the muffled voice coming through the door - immediately she rolled to the side, flinging her legs over the edge of the bed and rushing over. Hastily, she yanked the chair away and flung the door open to come face to face with Robin, dressed head to toe in palace maid clothes. Her heart fluttered and for a moment, Marian forgot about the danger of Robin being inside the palace, just happy to see her. But then, a guard turned the corner and Marian's senses returned, her face turning stern.

"What are you doing? Coming in this way?" Marian scolded, pulling her in by her wrist and shutting the door solidly behind them once more. "You could have so easily been caught - I..."

Robin pulled Marian in by her waist and kissed her on the forehead, silencing her words.

"I was worried about you and it wasn't late enough at night to scale the wall, I would have been seen." Robin rubbed comforting circles on Marian's back. "We didn't notice the candle right away because it was still light out, but once the sun started to set I told Willa that I couldn't wait any longer. So, I borrowed some clothes from the clothesline by the river and came in through the servants entrance in the back."

Marian opened her mouth to say something else but was silenced by a steadfast shake of Robin's head.

"Nobody saw me, my love." Robin took Marian's face in her hands and placed their foreheads together. "Now tell me, what's wrong?"

Marian took a shuddering breath and placed her hands over Robin's, squeezing her face even tighter. The pressure of Robin's touch on her cheeks gave Marian the courage to mutter out the depressing truth she'd been trying to shove into the back of her mind ever since she'd returned to her room.

"He's not giving me a choice."

Robin sighed, clearly not needing further explanation.

"He finally said it outright, did he?"

Marian huffed, closing her eyes and focusing only on the comforting scent of her lover. "I don't know what to do, Robin. He won't let me go."

Robin rubbed her back comfortingly in silence for a moment, nodding in understanding before making a decision.

"Well." Robin said resolutely. "Then, we will simply have to run away."

Marian huffed a laugh, a few errant tears slipping down her cheeks as her own words from yesterday were mirrored with such determination. "Even if we will be fugitives for the rest of our lives?"

Robin leaned back, leaving her hands on Marian's cheeks so she could look into her eyes.

"Even then."

Marian nodded, sniffling as the tears really began to flow. Leaning in, Marian brought their lips together in a wet kiss.

"Don't cry, my love." Robin whispered against her lips as she wiped Marian's tears away with her thumb.

Marian smiled into the kiss, tangling her fingers into her lover's hair as Robin backed them up against the bed. The backs of Marian's knees hit the mattress and she allowed herself to lay back, bringing Robin down onto the sheets with her. The weight of her body was comforting, quickly calming her down as she reveled in the feeling of Robin's hands running all over.

Everywhere Robin's fingers touched, a trail of goosebumps followed, causing Marian to arch up off the bed, desperate for Robin to touch her even more. Marian gripped Robin's hips, encouraging them to move, grinding down onto her.

Robin buried her face in Marian's neck, pulling at her dress until it was up off the ground and around her hips. Then, with a quick nip at her collarbone, Robin pushed onto her knees just off the bed and pulled Marian towards her by her thighs.

Marian gasped as Robin pulled her panties to the side and pressed an opened mouth kiss to her pussy, flicking her clit with her tongue as she pulled away. Marian buried a hand in Robin's hair, grinding up as Robin dove back in, eating her out like she was starving. Moving lower, Robin's tongue began to press inside as she brought a hand up, finger gently circling her clit as she fucked her with her tongue.

Marian covered her mouth with her free hand, unable to control the pleasured moans escaping her lips and not wanting anyone outside to hear. She felt as though she was on fire, unable to escape the liquid pleasure, pulsing through her veins each time Robin's tongue moved.

Moving once again, Robin's mouth wandered up to Marian's clit, sucking it gently as she pressed her fingers inside her lover, ever so slowly. Marian teetered on the edge of orgasm, gasping for breath until Robin finally began fucking her in earnest with her fingers. The change of pace mixed with the devastating suction on her clit sent Marian flying over the edge faster than she had ever thought herself capable.

Robin worked her through it as her thighs twitched around her head and Marian finally reached down, pulling Robin up for a kiss. Marian loved how she could taste herself on her lover's tongue and wasted no time at all reaching into Robin's pants, flipping her hand so that she was cupping her pussy in her palm and sliding her middle two fingers inside the wet heat.

Robin gasped, hips twitching forward desperately. Robin loved eating her out, sometimes coming with her tongue still tirelessly working, so Marian knew that it wouldn't take much for Robin to follow her into pleasure. Marian began tilting her wrist back and forth, gently thrusting her fingers in and out while rubbing her palm up against Robin's clit. Robin kissed her passionately, interrupted frequently with desperate gasps as she rubbed up against Marian's hand, only to silence her tantric moans once more with Marian's lips.

"Ah... Marian..." Robin gasped, her hips now moving erratically as she tightened around Marian's fingers.

"That's it, baby." Marian cooed, her free hand grasping at Robin's breast. "Come for me."

Robin's breath hitched and she began to shake. Marian pulled her fingers out, instead focusing all her attention on Robin's clit as she rode out her orgasm. She continued until Robin finally sighed, relaxing further into her touch and only then did she stop.

When Robin collapsed on top of her, Marian pulled her hand out and without breaking eye contact with her lover, sucked on her two middle fingers, watching as Robin's gaze darkened with desire.

"Oh shit." Robin murmured, kissing her once again. "Round two?"

Marian offered only a smile and curt nod before they were tangled up in each other once again.

Chapter Five

Marian lay naked beneath the covers, her head on Robin's chest as her lover traced shapes over her skin. Even though nothing had been fixed just yet, Marian already felt calmer. She didn't know how or when they were going to leave without risking exposing the Merry Men, but Robin seemed so sure of herself that she trusted that everything was going to be alright.

"You know." Robin mused, "it's a shame that we can't take gold directly from the palace. Give back some of those crazy taxes the Sheriff has been imposing recently."

Marian took a breath, ready to agree when she stopped - instead propping herself up on one elbow.

"Well, why can't we?"

Robin's eyebrows went up as she waited for Marian to continue. They'd avoided stealing directly from the palace in an effort to keep a low profile, but if they were going to be leaving anyway... Marian pulled her legs up underneath her and sat cross legged next to her lover, tossing her hair over her shoulder.

"Why not go out with a bang? The logistics aren't nearly as complicated as you might expect. The treasury is on the bottom level of the palace, next to the dungeons. It was built that way because theoretically that's the most secure part of the estate, but consequently that also means that it's directly next to the river."

Robin nodded slowly as understanding began dawning on her, shifting in the silk sheets of the bed.

"And the river runs through town..." Marian prompted, gesturing gently with her hand.

"So if we dumped the gold into the river," Robin grinned widely. "We could give it back to the people without having to distribute it ourselves, Marian! You're a genius."

Marian blushed as Robin lunged forward, wrapping her arms around Marian's waist, pressing excited kisses to her stomach. The movement caused the blankets covering them both to fall away, leaving them naked, the candlelight gently warming their skin.

"I don't know." Marian giggled. "I wouldn't say *genius*."

Robin sat up straight and cupped Marian's cheek with one hand. "I would."

Marian couldn't help the smile that overtook her face. The moon had just begun to rise and the shape of it through the window haloed Robin's hair like an iridescent crown. She looked beautiful, far more a queen in her own right than the King, John, or the Sheriff could ever be.

"With a haul like that, the Merry Men could move on - help another town, far away from here. And you and I, with some of that gold - could disappear, buy a cottage near the coast and never look back."

Before she allowed herself to become overcome with excitement, Marian paused, considering the implication. If Robin disappeared with her, she would be leaving the Merry Men and the life she built for herself behind.

"Are you sure?" Marian gazed into Robin's eyes, searching for any sign of hesitation. "The Merry Men are your life."

"*You* are my life, Marian." Robin replied, tilting her head, hair falling gently over her shoulder. "The Merry Men will always be family to me, but the possibility of living my life without you went out the window the day you crashed my hiding spot in that stable."

Marian laughed, her smile making her cheeks a little sore. Robin's smile was devastating and Marian knew in that moment that she could never deny that woman anything she asked for, so she nodded, finally allowing her excitement to take hold. Robin leaned forward once again, slotting their naked bodies together on the soft palace sheets.

"You and me, baby." Robin continued, pressing rapturous kisses to Marian's lips between words. "Let's get you that garden."

Marian knew the palace backwards and forwards; each hallway was as familiar to her as the lines of her own palm - which was what made this so easy.

It hadn't taken more than an hour or so for Marian to draw out and walk Robin through a detailed schematic of the palace to bring back to the Merry Men.

"All the residences are up on the third floor, including Prince

John's. The second floor is dedicated primarily to studies, meeting rooms, and areas to host guests, and the ground floor is where you'll find the kitchen and a majority of the servant's quarters." Marian pointed out each area on the map as she spoke.

"The servant entrance that you came in yesterday is right here." Marian placed her finger on the door located in the back of the kitchen. "The cook needs to come and go to gather water from the river, pull wood from the pile out back, and dispose of garbage so it's very rarely locked.

The good news is that the staircase leading further downstairs into the vaults and dungeon is right around the corner, here." Marian looked up at Robin, checking for understanding.

"And the bad news?" Robin grinned playfully.

"Well, the top of the staircase isn't guarded, but right when you reach the bottom of the stairs, there are guards sitting at posts here and here preventing passage from anyone wandering in."

Robin nodded, leaning forward onto her knees. "So, we either need a reason to be there or find another way in."

"Exactly." Marian nodded. "I've never been inside the vault itself, but from what I can tell, there aren't any windows or openings leading to the outside. So it would be safe to assume that there's a limited supply of air in the actual treasure chamber."

Robin pursed her lips in consideration. "So the major obstacles here are getting inside and getting the gold out into the river without suffocating."

"Yes." Marian smirked. "But once we figure out those two things, we are in the clear."

"Oh, is that all?" Robin teased, leaning back on the bed and crossing her legs.

Marian took another quick look at the map before turning to Robin, a mischievous grin on her face.

"What is it?" Robin asked, watching her carefully.

"So, I know that the Merry Men tend to fly underneath the radar, but if we are preparing to vacate the area anyway, I don't see why we couldn't... make a little bit more commotion."

Marian made her way down the hallway, her steps echoing loudly against the brick walls. Shortly after their conversation, Robin had donned her servant's clothes once more and taken off down the hallway back towards the kitchens.

The plan was simple, but did require some time to pull together, so in the meantime, as she waited, Marian readied her go bag and prayed that Prince John would be reasonable. She didn't know how long a royal wedding would take to prepare, but her hope was that it wouldn't happen in the next three days. Even as the third son, the King would likely want their wedding to be bigger than a small, intimate gathering at the chapel. And that information alone was the only thing keeping her panic from bubbling over and drowning her where she stood.

As she made her way down the stairs to meet the Prince for dinner, her heart rate jackrabbited. Despite all of her self assurances and faith in the Merry Men, she couldn't help but feel uneasy about her part in all of this. Part of her felt guilty about lying to Prince John - but a larger part of her anxiety came from the idea that he would catch her in a lie. She was terrified that her racing pulse would give her away, that somehow, Prince

John would see her blood pumping beneath her skin and know that she was being shifty.

The Merry Men needed the next three days to pool their resources, gather the necessary tools, and pack up the camp; if Marian fucked that up for them, they'd be caught with their pants down and no way to defend themselves. What's more, she wouldn't get to see Robin until after the heist was over - so in truth, if something happened between now and then, she wouldn't actually know until it was too late.

Their typical methods of communication would be out of order for the foreseeable future and since it was too risky for Robin to come back to the palace and Marian couldn't leave - Marian was essentially in the dark. The Prince's eyes were on her always, and she had to keep those eyes turned inwards and away from the woods at all costs.

As she entered the dining hall, she slowed her pace at the sound of a pair of chatting voices echoing through the empty chamber. She recognized one to be Prince John right away, but couldn't quite put her finger on the second speaker from her current distance, so she continued forward, investigating further. Marian walked quietly through the dining hall, careful to keep her footfalls as light as she could as she approached the south entrance.

Getting closer, the voices became more and more clear. Marian paused behind a pillar.

"They've been getting lazy, you can't be too lenient with them, Your Highness, or they'll walk all over you."

Marian grimaced, she knew that voice. Peering out from behind the pillar, Marian pursed her lips and quieted her breathing; sure enough, standing several feet away from the Prince, was the one person Marian had wanted to avoid more than anyone else over these next couple of days. There, standing in the entryway with the Prince was Nottingham's very own Sheriff.

She wanted to flee, but as she attempted a retreat, the bottom of her dress rustled against a nearby plant and the conversation stopped. Clenching her teeth, she made a hasty decision, not wanting to let them find her spying and stepped from the safety of her hiding place. Marian smiled, tilting her head in an effort to make herself seem smaller and less threatening as she'd been taught by the court ladies. Fortunately, it seemed to work - disarming the Sheriff and resulting only in a surprised look from the Prince.

"Ah, my Lady." Philip grinned, tilting his head in a bow. Marian had to physically restrain herself from taking a step back, away from the slimy man. Towering above her in height and stature, the Sheriff of Nottingham was not a subtle man - the increases in taxes that Robin had talked about earlier had significantly padded his personal pocket and he clearly felt no shame in showing it. Instead of the standard Sheriff's uniform that he had been wearing for the better part of 20 years, Philip had upgraded his clothes to an ostentatious red and orange shirt with puffy sleeves and a purple striped hat with a feather poking from the top. It was distasteful to say the least and Marian had to physically hold back the grimace that naturally curled her lip.

"Sheriff." Marian gritted her teeth and forced a small curtsey. "To what do we owe this pleasure?"

The Sheriff adjusted his belt, rocking back on his heels as he nodded - sword hanging heavy on his hip.

"I was just informing his Highness about how some of his subjects are trying to skimp out on taxes lately. But don't worry, I made sure to educate them on their dedication to the Crown."

Marian's gaze flicked up to Prince John, who was watching the Sheriff with a stoic face before pursing her lips in a tight smile. She knew that face, she'd seen it on him many times when they sat together with their instructor as children. Prince John was searching desperately for an out.

"I see. Well, I'm so sorry to interrupt, but I'm afraid that the Prince and I have a rather important matter to discuss over dinner."

Prince John glanced over, seemingly surprised at Marian's announcement but did not contradict her, a grateful softness to his eyes.

"Yes." John nodded. "Thank you for the report, but I'm afraid we will have to continue this at a later date."

The Sheriff's face soured but he did not protest, instead sliding into a bow directed at both of them.

"Of course, always a pleasure." Philip's eyes raked up Marian's figure predatorily, sending shudders down her spine, before nodding once more to the Prince and skulking from the room.

Marian turned back to the Prince, unsurprised to see his eyes already locked on her. His face was less stony than it had been a few moments ago and despite everything, Marian relaxed.

"Why is he still the Sheriff, again?" Marian asked, heading into the dining hall. John followed her, and as she sat down, her eyes met his across the table.

"My father appointed him." John picked up his wine glass, taking a sip. "I've never been the biggest fan of his, but he gets the job done so it's frankly, not worth the fight it would cause with my father to replace him."

Marian pushed some vegetables around on her plate as she

wondered errantly if that was how he felt about their impending nuptials as well.

"Can I take it that your presence here tonight means that you've come around?"

Marian swallowed as she tried not to shake her head no, instead lifting her gaze and straightening her posture.

"I suppose so."

John sighed but didn't push for a more concrete answer, instead focusing his attention on his plate. For one brief moment, Marian thought that would be the end of it and she could stew on her lie in silence, but of course that's not how things played out.

"A spring wedding would be nice."

Marian expected to feel a sense of relief move through her as the Prince set the date for several months from now, but mostly she felt heavy as the Prince continued.

"That's your favorite season, right? Spring?"

Marian's throat tightened as unexpected tears began gathering at the corners of her eyes.

"Yes, your Highness." Marian choked out, covering her emotions with a short cough. As much as she didn't want to marry him, they'd still grown up together - it was strange, outside Robin and the Merry Men, John was the closest thing to a family she'd ever had. She knew he was lonely, cooped up in the palace all the time, so far from his father and brothers - but no matter how much it hurt, she just couldn't bring herself to give him what he wanted.

"I know this is... a lot to ask of you." Prince John continued, his voice measured. "But, I think that we *can* find happiness together - long term, I mean. My mother married my father before ever meeting him and even she eventually grew fond of him; you and I grew up together, so perhaps it's not completely out of the question that we too, could fall in love someday."

Marian took a deep breath and looked up at John with sad eyes. She would never be able to love him the way he needed, and part of her hoped that he knew that - so he could temper his expectations. But despite everything...

"You know that I *do* love you, right?"

John's face softened once more, but this time his expression was laced with a sort of melancholy that Marian was not accustomed to seeing on him.

"Yes." He replied quietly. "I know."

Chapter Six

The morning of the heist, Marian woke up both excited and full of dread. The night before she'd received a message in the form of a raven at her window with a note carefully tied to his leg. It wasn't long and there was no to or from line just in case it got intercepted, but when Marian unfurled the note - she knew exactly what it meant.

Let's get you that garden. 12. Tomorrow.

She'd barely slept that night and kept checking her go bag over and over again until she finally had to force herself to lie down. She needed to be fresh in the morning, ready to go, and she wouldn't be of any use to anybody if she was falling asleep during the raid in the afternoon.

She hadn't felt this anxious about a heist since the very first time Robin had invited her to participate. In fact, she'd been so nervous that when she walked up to distract the mark, she'd thrown up all over his shoes. Robin had laughed and everyone had made fun of her for months afterwards, but she had actually managed to distract the man, so nobody could tell her that she hadn't done her part. Since then, she'd gotten far more accustomed to the rhyme and rhythm of each plot the Merry Men came up with and could now get through her part without losing her lunch.

However, this was far bigger than anything any of them had attempted in the past and the consequences for failure were significantly higher. So, for the first time in a long time, Marian felt her stomach twist as she watched the clock tick closer and closer to go time.

At a quarter to noon, Marian grabbed her bag, hid it in a basket of dirty laundry, and started off towards the first floor. She just had to get her go bag out of the palace without it being seen and stash it somewhere she could easily get to it once shit hit the fan. Everything she cared to bring with her into her new life was in that bag - so she had to hide it well. After much thought and deliberation, Marian had decided that right outside, by the washing was her best chance. The bridge, leading across the river and into the outer courtyards was sparsely guarded and unassuming enough that it hardly warranted a second look from anyone passing, so in truth - it was the perfect spot.

Surprised by how smoothly everything was going so far, Marian hurried down the stairs and turned the corner towards the servants quarters. She was almost to the kitchen when fate decided to check her in the worst possible way.

"Lady Marian."

Marian paused, looking back over her shoulder as her ladies maid hurried over from further down the hallway where she had been speaking to none other than the Sheriff.

"Why are you carrying your own laundry? I would have brought it down later!"

Ella was only trying to help, but in that moment, Marian saw their entire plan flash before her eyes. The Sheriff was early, had the Merry Men gotten to his delivery in time? Marian swallowed, her grip tightening on the basket as the Sheriff raised an eyebrow in her direction.

Ella moved to take the basket, but at the last moment, Marian side-stepped her with a gentle shake of her head.

"That's quite alright, Ella. I know that you have other duties and there was something specific I wanted to wear later today, so I decided to just bring it down to Portia myself."

Ella furrowed her brow, extending her hands once again. "It's no problem, really - I was just heading that way myself."

Marian felt the Sheriff's eyes on her as she realized that there was no way for her to get out of this that didn't look suspicious. So, instead she gave Ella a tight-lipped smile and handed over the basket.

"Thank you." Marian murmured. "I have some specific instructions for her so if you wouldn't mind just placing it with the other baskets outside, I'll be by in a moment to talk to her."

This seemed to appease Ella, as she nodded and took off - seemingly equally as excited to get away from the Sheriff as she was to do her duty. Marian watched, full of anxiety, as her basket - go bag stashed strategically at the bottom - was carried around the corner and out of her sight.

"I hear that congratulations are in order." The Sheriff's grating voice, now closer than it had been before, rang through Marian's ears, forcing her to turn back towards the man.

"Is that so?" Marian smiled as genuinely as she could. "What ever for?"

"Your engagement." Philip pulled back his lips in an unsettling grin. "Of course I had been wondering when the Prince would finally put his foot down. You're getting rather up there in age and of course the King has been anxious to continue his bloodline."

Marian hated the way he looked at her - she'd seen that look in every nobleman she'd come across since she'd been old enough to understand what men wanted from her. He was undressing her with his eyes and suddenly, Marian yearned for the pants and leather vests that the Merry Men wore in the woods instead of the flowing linen that hugged her curves and emphasized her figure.

"Ah, yes." Marian nodded, trying her best not to slouch away from his gaze. "Thank you, for the congratulations, I mean."

"We were beginning to worry that the Prince didn't have the balls to do what had to be done."

Marian's blood ran cold and she couldn't help the scowl that crossed her face. "Oh? And what exactly do you mean by that?"

The Sheriff laughed, loudly and grating as he adjusted the sword on his hip. "Defensive, are we?"

Marian tried to soften her gaze, but only succeeded in pursing her lips in response. Unfortunately, her response only emboldened the Sheriff, a sickly grin spreading across his face.

"Listen, 'Lady' Marian." Philip stepped forward into Marian's space. She wanted to retreat, but something inside her forced her to stand her ground, despite the Sheriff's cologne rich scent choking her as she breathed. "You may have the misconception of status, living in the palace and growing up alongside the Prince, but I was here the night you were brought in off the streets. I know what you are."

Marian gritted her teeth, all illusions of civility finally falling away completely. "Oh? And what am I, exactly?"

The Sheriff huffed, a satisfied grin pinned to his face as he leaned down to get eye to eye with Marian. "Nobody."

Marian forced herself to maintain eye contact despite every fiber of her being telling her to run away. She needed to get back to the servants quarters and ensure that she hid her go bag, but she knew that if she retreated now he would only follow her - and she couldn't have that.

"You're just a peasant off the street that the King took pity on. Living here for years, acting like you have a choice in whether or not the Prince takes you as his wife. I've watched you for over a decade, acting like you're too good for this place - running away and spitting in the face of the kindness the King bestowed upon you all those years ago."

The Sheriff stood up straight, making no move to step back, instead looking down on Marian from above and forcing her to tilt her head nearly to the limit to maintain eye contact.

"If I were the Prince, I wouldn't have waited. If you were meant to be my wife, I would have taken you whenever I wanted, as many times as I wanted. You've had a nice rack on you, ever since you were 16 - that's old enough to marry. If you weren't betrothed to the Prince, I would have fucked you bloody every chance I got years ago."

Marian clenched her fists, ready to lash out when she was saved by a voice from down the hall.

"Sheriff, Sir. We have the delivery for you."

Marian refused to break eye contact until Philip was forced to turn around, but once his back was to her, Marian felt all the adrenaline drain from her body - leaving her feeling faint.

However, despite the shake in her hands and knees, Marian

forced herself to stay upright. Peering around the Sheriff's massive figure, Marian let out a small breath of relief at a familiar face. Among the two other deliverymen and the massive wooden box, stood Willa - looking concerned but calm.

Marian nodded as discreetly as she could to indicate that she was alright and noted how Willa's shoulders relaxed as she understood. Coming back to her senses, Marian turned tail and took off back towards the kitchen.

Turning the corner and shutting the kitchen door behind her, Marian glanced around, making eye contact with one of the sous chefs.

"Did you see Ella come this way?" Marian asked as nonchalantly as she could, hiding her shaking hands from view.

"Yes, ma'am. She headed out back not five minutes ago." The sous chef pointed to the servant's entrance with his wooden spoon.

Good, Marian thought. Now, she could only hope that Ella had followed her instructions and not tampered with the basket in any way. Hurrying out the back entrance, Marian took the dirt path down to the river, shaded by the shadow of the Palace.

Ella was nowhere to be seen and for a moment, Marian panicked - head on a swivel as she desperately looked for her basket. She was being far more conspicuous than she'd originally intended, but luckily Portia didn't seem to be around either.

Making her way through the baskets and piles of sheets on the wooden dock, Marian tried to remain low and out of sight. She tried to convince herself that even if her go bag was lost, everything would still be alright, but when she finally laid eyes on her basket, she almost sobbed in relief. Scrambling over to it,

Marian dropped to her knees, tossing clothes out until her hand finally touched the leather of her bag.

Marian dropped her head, hand wrapping around the shoulder strap as she finally allowed herself to breathe again. Quickly, Marian looked around to ensure that she was alone before pulling the bag out and hurrying over to the bank underneath the dock. There she found the cluster of rocks that she'd strategically placed several nights ago and hid her bag in the middle.

She was running late in her tasks because of the Sheriff, but Willa had just arrived with the package - so if she hurried, she should still be able to meet her in time.

Checking once more that she wasn't being watched, Marian hurried to her feet and started off towards the gardens, skirting the Palace walls. The Prince was meeting with Duke Charles of Thoresby Hall to discuss the agricultural plan for this quarter so she didn't need to worry about accidentally running into him, but there were still servants everywhere.

Marian hadn't used this path for an escape in years, so she truly hoped that the Prince had stopped ordering patrols in this area, but she couldn't be sure. Rounding the corner, Marian pressed her back up against the cold stone, peeking around the bush blocking her view into the gardens. For a moment, her heart seized up when she saw no one; terrified that she'd missed them coming out, Marian almost stepped out of her hiding spot and onto the path but stopped as she heard a door open.

"Fuckin' heavy those crates are."

"What did you expect? They're full of gold you half-wit."

Marian let out a shuddering breath as Willa and the two transporters exited the building. Whistling like Robin had taught her years ago, Marian alerted Willa to her presence with her practiced wood pigeon call.

"You jack-asses go on." Willa nonchalantly shooed the others off. "The Sheriff asked that I hang around until he's done."

One of the two men paused, crossing his arms. "Why only you?"

Willa's face devolved into irritation that Marian was sure she wasn't faking and placed her hands on her hips.

"Oh?" Willa tilted her head. "Do you want to wait around for the Sheriff to finish fucking whatever servant girl he finds so *you* can carry his take of the taxes?"

Marian bit her lip, but didn't need to wait long to see the resignation in the eyes of the two others as they exchanged a glance.

"Yeah, alright." The first man shook his head, punching the other in the shoulder. "Let's fucking go."

Willa waited until the two were out of sight before turning towards Marian's hiding spot and walking slowly over. With one more look to ensure she wasn't being followed, Willa dodged behind the bush, joining Marian in the grass.

"Here." Willa reached into the bag she was carrying, pulling out a pair of pants and shirt. "Get changed, everyone's in position and once it starts, there won't be a second to pause."

Marian nodded, hastily pulling the pants on underneath her dress before yanking it over her head and tossing it to the side. Quickly, she picked up the shirt and pulled it on, tucking it into her pants.

"Is everything alright?" Marian asked, settling back on the balls of her feet. "Did he suspect?"

"No." Willa shook her head. "Everything went according to plan."

Just then, like a sign from God - a massive explosion rung through the Palace, shaking the stones of the courtyard and sending every bird within a several mile radius up into the sky.

Willa nodded resolutely, standing and offering Marian her hand.

"Let's go."

Chapter Seven

Willa and Marian took off in the direction of the explosion, leaving Marian's discarded dress in the dirt behind the bushes. Now that the initial shock of the explosion had worn off, people were beginning to mobilize. As the pair dashed past the Palace, Marian caught glimpses of the guards in the barracks, hastily grabbing their weapons and donning armor as quickly as they could.

As they turned the corner back towards the river, Marian's eyes grew wide at the sight of the massive hole that had been blown in the side of the wall. The initial blast had already sent a great deal of gold and treasure flying into the torrents of the river, already being swept away into town by the current. However, as they approached, Marian watched as barrels and chests, presumably filled with treasure, were pushed off the, now building cliffside, and into the river.

At this distance, she couldn't quite recognize who was doing the pushing, but it seemed that everything was going according to plan. Even so, Marian was anxious to lay eyes on Robin. She'd almost had a heart attack when Robin told

Marian that she planned to be inside the box along with the explosives that were going to be smuggled in.

Robin assured her that they weren't unstable enough to go off on their own and that she would keep the flint and steel each individually wrapped in cloth, in *separate* pockets until she was safely out. Despite this, however, Marian's head was still reeling with everything that could have possibly gone wrong. Robin could have been standing too close to the blast when it went off, or she could have forgotten to cover her ears in time and gone permanently deaf from the echoes of the blast inside the treasure chamber, or a million other things.

As they approached, Willa, seemingly feeling Marian's anxiety, nudged her and pointed up at the giant hole as the smoke cleared.

Marian took a deep breath of relief as Robin made herself known, waving from atop a piece of rubble.

"See?" Willa panted as they ran. "I told you she'd be fine."

Despite her relief, Marian continued running; they only had a short amount of time to do what they had to do before the guards showed up and then they had to get the hell out of here. Willa pulled an empty sack out from her bag and handed it to Marian before dropping to her knee right below the edge of the explosion zone, ready to give Marian a boost up.

Marian scrambled up into the treasure room, incredibly thankful for her change of clothes, and after pausing only a beat to look Robin over to make sure she didn't have any major wounds, she scurried over to a pile of gold coins next to the locked door and began scooping them into her bag.

The Merry Men had agreed to spend their energy getting as much treasure into the river as they could, mostly chests and barrels, anything that could float and Robin had tasked Marian to build up their little nest egg out of some of the treasure too far from the edge to be sent into the river in time.

She could hear the guards trying everything they could to open the door, not having realized until that moment that Willa had taken their keys. Marian didn't let it bother her, as the longer it took for them to realize they needed to go around, the more time the Merry Men would have to dump treasure.

Marian had just finished fitting as much gold as she could in the satchel and was about to start helping the rest of the group when the room suddenly shook with a violent slam. Marian turned back around to face the door just in time for another solid hit to rattle the door nearly off its hinges. There weren't any siege weapons in the dungeons, so as the door continued to groan and creak - Marian found herself increasingly concerned about what could possibly be attempting to break through.

"Can they get through that?" Joanna's voice rang out - a touch panicked.

Marian whipped her head around to find Robin, standing atop a pile of cups, a wild smile plastered to her face.

"Well, we're about to find out!"

With one final creak, the door gave way, revealing the hulking figure of Sheriff Phillip. He had to hunch down to step through the doorway and once he did, his eyes landed directly on Marian.

With an animalistic growl, the Sheriff pointed a finger and shouted. "You fucking bitch! I should have known."

Marian scrambled backwards, tripping over a pile of coins as he began moving towards her. But before he could get too close, a dagger flew across the room, slicing his cheek and sending him stumbling backwards a couple of paces. Furious, Phillip whipped his head around locking eyes with Robin.

"Please don't call the love of my life a fucking bitch." Robin asked politely, reaching for her sword. "It's rude."

The Sheriff frowned, taking in the crowd before him for a moment before breaking out in a deep, unsettling laugh.

"I didn't fucking believe it, but that stupid cunt was right. You are just a bunch of bitches" Philip placed a hand on his own sword, seemingly waiting for Robin to make a move.

"You hear that, my Dear?" Robin called over to Marian. "Seems like our mate Douglas had more balls than we gave him credit for!"

Marian slowly moved to stand, but as she did, the Sheriff whipped his head back her way and drew his sword with a lunge.

"You sneaky bitch! I'll kill you and then fuck your corpse!" The Sheriff howled, hurtling towards her. Marian shielded her face with her arms and pushed backwards as far as she could on the ground waiting for impact. But it never came.

Instead she heard a clash of swords and when she opened her eyes, she saw Robin, blocking the Sheriff's path to her. Marian crawled behind a chest and whipped around, watching as Robin and Phillip went head to head.

The Sheriff was bigger and far stronger, but Robin was quicker - whenever the Sheriff would raise his sword to bring it down she was long gone by the time it crashed into the stone floor. Unfortunately, that meant that Robin couldn't get too close - the Sheriff's sword was massive, with a frightening range, one upswing from the ground could catch and incapacitate Robin in an instant.

Even so, Marian still had faith in Robin - she would outmaneuver him.

Unfortunately, in the confusion, it seemed that everyone

else had forgotten that the vault door was now wide open. The two guards who had been with the Sheriff had already slipped inside and were fighting Willa and Hester on the lip of the explosion point, but now, Marian heard the loud rattling of armor making its way down the staircase.

They had been banking on the fact that the guards would have a difficult time climbing up into the vault with their armor but now that they could just walk right in, they were in danger of being overwhelmed. Standing shakily on her trembling legs, Marian ran to the entrance in hopes of shutting the door, but it was unsalvageable. It had been busted nearly off its hinges and the wood surrounding the lock was completely shattered beyond recognition.

Marian willed herself to think in the midst of the shouts and clashing swords when she stopped, her gaze on a pile of crates to the left of the door. Hurriedly she ran around to the side, braced her hands on one of the lower crates and pushed.

Nothing.

It didn't even budge; whatever was in these crates was solid, heavy, and unmoving. Desperately, Marian took a few steps back and ran, full force into the boxes - whimpering as her shoulder slammed into the side, but no luck.

The guards were coming down the hallway, if they got inside, the Merry Men would quickly be overwhelmed. Marian spun around, desperately searching for anything that might help when her gaze landed on a sword. It was clearly ceremonial and blunt along the edges, but she wasn't planning on using it to fight.

Marian rushed over to the sword, pulling it out of the pile it had found its home in and hurried back over to the boxes, shoving the tip of the sword underneath and pushing down.

There was more movement than there had been when she was pushing directly, but it barely wobbled.

"Come on." Marian hissed under her breath as she placed her entire weight on the far end of the sword, pulsing in a rhythmic fashion. At first, it made very little difference, but then with each push, the stack of crates swayed more and more. Sweat dripped from her brow and into her eyes as the hilt of the sword dug into her ribs with each push. Finally, the crates at the top rocked unsteadily, and at last the bottom crate gave way, sending Marian crashing to the ground.

Marian snapped her head up, watching in desperation just as the first of the guards started to make their way into the treasure room. But with a final groan, the heavy crates crashed to the ground, crushing the first couple of knights and effectively blocking the entrance.

Marian dropped her head with an overdue sigh of relief.

"Yes!" Willa cried out as she kicked one of the guards off the side and into the river. "Great job, Marian!"

Marian grinned widely, instinctively seeking out Robin but when she found her, the smile was wiped from her face. The Sheriff had her pinned down on her back as she struggled to keep his sword from slicing her neck.

"No." Marian whispered, jumping into action, scrambling up off the floor. As she moved, she ran over to a crossbow that a guard had dropped on his way inside and snatched it up, praying that it was still loaded. She wasn't a fighter, she knew that, Robin knew that, and even the Sheriff knew that. But she would never sit idly by as Robin was beheaded.

So with shaking hands, Marian hoisted the crossbow, bracing it as well as she could on her arm. It was too heavy for her and she's never shot something like it before, but at that moment, none of those things mattered.

"Hey Phillip!" Marian shouted, her face screwed up in a scowl. With Robin still pinned beneath him, he turned and Marian saw the exact moment he registered what was happening. His eyes went wide and Marian watched as his face paled.

"Fuck you." Marian loosed the arrow and while she wasn't the best shot, she was at point blank range. The arrow catapulted out of the crossbow and lodged itself in the Sheriff's skull, directly through his cheekbone and out the back of his head.

Robin took advantage of the moment and shoved the sword to the side, kicking him away just as the Sheriff's body toppled onto the stone floor.

Marian's hands shook violently as she gripped the crossbow - Robin was fine, and that was all that mattered. She distantly heard some of the Merry Men cheering, but it was all drowned out by the view of blood pooling around the Sheriff's body, staining the nearby treasures red.

"...ian. Marian?" Marian came back as Robin gripped her shoulders, gently taking the crossbow and tossing it to the floor with a clatter.

"Robin?" Tears gathered at the corners of Marian's eyes. She had hated that man, he'd just threatened her earlier that day even before he'd known about her involvement. He surely would have killed her had he gotten the chance, but even so, she couldn't help how the feeling of taking a life overwhelmed her.

"Yes, baby." Robin smiled, bringing Marian into her embrace. "You did so good, you saved my life."

"I did?" Marian murmured, tears streaming silently down her face.

"Yes, baby." Robin squeezed her, holding her together as her body threatened to fall apart at the seams. "You did so amazing. I would have been a goner if you hadn't stepped in. Come on, let's get you out of here."

Marian nodded, looking once more at the lifeless body lying on the vault floor. Then, she let Robin pull her away, towards the ragged edges of the building. Robin dropped down first, holding out her arms for Marian, but before she could jump, someone gently took her hand.

Marian flinched, adrenaline still pumping through her body but relaxed as she turned to see Willa, looking at her with an expression of profound gratitude.

"Thank you for saving her, Marian." Willa squeezed Marian's hand comfortingly and Marian found herself smiling back.

"Always." Marian nodded, allowing herself to be pulled into a brief hug before Willa helped her sit on the edge and hop into Robin's arms.

"Come on, let's go." Robin set Marian's feet on the ground and took her hand. "Where'd you hide your bag?"

"Over by the laundry." Marian gestured as Robin picked up her own bag that had been stashed in the reeds near the river by one of the Merry Men before the explosion.

"Alright." Robin waved a short goodbye to the rest of the crew and took Marian's hand in her own. Then, with one final grin, she took off, leading them toward the laundry and away from the scene of the crime.

Chapter Eight

The laundry area was blessedly empty, as Marian led Robin over to the bridge. Once they were out of sight, Robin dropped them down into a crouch and took Marian's face in her hands.

"Are you alright?" Robin's eyes darted all over her face, searching for any sort of scratch or injury. Marian allowed herself to be doted on, taking the opportunity to catch her breath and refocus on the mission.

"I'm fine, I'm not the one who was trapped in a brawl." Marian tried playing it off, but Robin didn't let go, gaze softening.

"That's not what I mean, baby."

Marian's bottom lip trembled as tears pooled at the corners of her eyes once more. Marian brought her hands up to Robin's face, touching their foreheads together.

"I couldn't let him kill you." Marian's voice wavered as she held back tears. "But I've never... there was so much blood..."

"I know." Robin pulled Marian in, cradling her head and pressing kisses into her hair. "But you did so good, now we just have to get to the church - there are some horses waiting for us there. Then this will all be over and the only thing you'll need to worry about is what you'll want to plant first in our garden."

Marian nodded, lifting her head and leaning in for a quick kiss before shakily making her way to her feet once again and ducking underneath the bridge. She hurried across the shifting pebbles of the river bank and over to the pile of rocks that hid her bag, but when she reached behind it, her heart dropped.

It wasn't there.

"Fuck." Marian pulled her hand back, shuffling to the side and trying again. "My bag... it's..."

"Looking for this?"

Marian's heart dropped into her stomach as a familiar voice called from the across the river bank. Frozen in place, Marian stared at the pile of rocks, willing her bag to just *be there*, willing for any possible way to escape this interaction. But when one didn't come, she took a deep breath and turned.

She didn't need to look to know who was standing there, but she did anyway. As she turned, she came face to face with Prince John, his expression was unreadable as he held her bag in one hand.

He wasn't supposed to be here. Despite everything, Marian wasn't ready to see the look of betrayal on his face.

"I-" Marian started before being cut off by a single finger held up by Prince John's free hand. He clearly wasn't ready to hear what she had to say, and she wasn't ready to have this conversation, but they were running out of time.

"Marian." Robin's voice was low and wary as she side-stepped carefully under the cover of the bridge. "Do you need me to take care of him?"

"What?" Marian turned to Robin who was reaching for her

sword once more and huffed a frustrated breath. "No! Stand down."

Robin watched her for a moment before standing back up straight, hand moving away from her sheath. John wasn't there to hurt her, he couldn't be, Marian refused to believe it, but even so, she was at a loss for how to handle this impromptu meeting.

Marian swallowed, closing her eyes for a moment before taking a deep breath and meeting gazes with the Prince once more.

"Sire, I can explain..."

"Come now, Marian. I think we are at the point where we can speak plainly with each other, don't you?" Prince John's voice blew past her attempt at cordiality, filled with unmasked hurt.

Marian swallowed but nodded, chewing her lip nervously. It broke her heart to hear him that way, the last time she'd heard that level of pain in his voice, had been when his mother died. She knew she should run, use his confusion to her advantage and flee, but regardless of everything, she just couldn't. She owed him the truth.

"John." Marian hadn't called him that in years, not since they were children playing in the royal gardens together. "This is..."

"Robin Hood of Sherwood Forest?" Prince John finished for her. "Yes, I gathered that much. I just never expected her to be-"

"A woman?" Robin spoke up.

John's gaze moved from Marian to Robin for a moment before nodding curtly.

He'd gotten to the bag before she could, he had to have seen their interaction; Marian wasn't sure whether or not she should feel relieved. On one hand, now he knew - he knew why she'd been so resistant to marry him, but on the other hand, it felt worse than she thought it would, him finding out this way.

"So," John looked back over to Marian. "You're..."

"Yes." Marian couldn't help the way the word came out as an apology. "John, I'm sorry, I just couldn't... I'm not..."

"You love her." The words sounded so resolute coming out of Prince John's mouth and it was the finality of it all that broke Marian again, streams of tears running down her cheeks. Through the misty haze of her tears, she saw the Prince's face soften slightly - she hadn't cried in front of him for quite some time.

"I do." Marian nodded, the words catching on her throat. However, despite her tears, she couldn't help but feel lighter. For the first time in a long time, Marian didn't feel as though she was speaking to the Prince, but rather, John, the boy she'd grown up with.

John paused for a moment, taking in everything before Marian saw the fight leave his stance as his shoulders relaxed, vice grip on her bag loosened.

"You tried to tell me." John nodded, brow furrowed. "But I didn't listen."

Marian pursed her lips, she hated how defeated he sounded. "You were only doing as your father asked."

"Yes, but..." John paused, looking at the bag in his hand. "I can't help but feel that we wouldn't be having this conversation right now 50 feet from a giant hole in the palace if I'd just let you go."

Marian let out a short burst of air in relief. "Perhaps that's true, sorry about that, by the way."

John huffed out a laugh, shrugging his shoulders. "It's not like I'm going to be the one who has to fix it anyway."

Marian stood in silence, listening to the trickling of the water over rocks - there was so much she could say, so much she felt she had to say... but there simply wasn't the time. So instead, she just settled for:

"You know I do love you, right?"

John lifted his gaze in surprise.

"You don't hate me?" John murmured, his expression conflicted.

"I could never hate you, John. You're my family."

John sighed and Marian slowly approached, stepping through the shallow areas of the river under the bridge. She could sense Robin tensing up as she got closer but her attention was fully on John. Once across, she paused, looking at her bag, still in his hand.

John followed her gaze and nodded resolutely. "You're still leaving, aren't you?"

"If you let me." Marian replied quietly, extending her hand for the bag. She hoped that this would be enough for him to finally let her go, but she really couldn't be sure. So instead of pushing it, she waited - hoping desperately that he would give her his blessing.

The world seemed to stand still as John considered Marian's hand, the sounds of the river muting their conversation from those not under the bridge with them. Then, finally, John handed Marian the bag.

"I can't protect you from repercussions from this. My father will want the head of whoever blew a hole in the castle."

"I know." Marian gripped the strap tightly, gaze never leaving John's. "And, you should know..."

Marian swallowed. "The Sheriff, he's dead."

John's brow furrowed in confusion as he looked to Robin for a moment.

"No." Marian continued with a shake of her head, taking John's hand in hers. "It was me."

"I see." John took a deep breath and for a moment, Marian thought that he was going to take back his blessing, but despite the potential consequences she simply couldn't stand the thought of him finding out anything else about her that she didn't tell him herself. However, much to Marian's surprise, John just gave her hand a squeeze and nodded. "Well, that's one less conversation I'll have to have with my father, I suppose."

Marian's jaw dropped and Robin made a choking noise that seemed to be a mix between a gasp and a chuckle. John rubbed his thumb over Marian's hand and nodded one final time before pulling Marian into a tight hug.

With a shuddering breath, Marian hugged him back, squeezing her eyes shut in an attempt to preserve this moment in her memory.

"Thank you, John." Marian whispered, pulling back and placing a single kiss to the Prince's cheek.

John nodded and stepped back, out of Marian's reach.

"I won't tell my father it was you, but if he finds out on his own - there's nothing I can do to protect you, you know that, right?"

Marian nodded. "I do."

John's gaze softened once more and with one final look, he turned and began making his way back to the castle, likely to "discover" that the Sheriff had been killed and do all the things a Prince was supposed to do after being robbed.

Watching his figure grow smaller and smaller, Marian found

herself feeling strangely sentimental. Part of Marian's heart hurt for him, knowing that she would be leaving him to deal with all of this alone, but she also knew that she couldn't stay.

Robin's hand found hers and she tore her gaze from John's retreating figure, instead looking over at her lover, her future. Robin smiled gently, giving her hand a squeeze.

"Come on." Robin murmured. "We have to go."

Marian nodded and adjusted the strap on her shoulder before they took off into the outer courtyards towards the church.

Just as they arrived in the outskirts of town, a horn sounded from the palace walls - likely announcing the death of the Sheriff. However, despite this, Marian remained strangely calm as she knew that John wouldn't be sending guards after them immediately. But even so, it was still strange - being so at ease after everything that had transpired in the past couple of hours.

As they rounded the corner to the church, Marian caught sight of the Friar, holding the reins of two horses outside the cemetery. Robin jogged over to greet him and Marian chanced a look back, just for a moment before following suit.

Robin said a quick goodbye to the Friar and tied their bags to each of their respective saddles before helping Marian up onto her horse. Then, after ensuring her lover was settled, Robin swung into her own saddle and the pair started off. There wasn't much town left to ride through and soon enough the road transitioned from cobblestone to packed dirt and the odd farm turned to rolling hills in every direction. By the time they stopped to eat, Nottingham was only a tiny collection of miniatures in the distance.

Marian took a bite of her bread as she sat at the top of the hill, considering the view. She had never been so far from Nottingham before, it was surreal looking at it so far away. They were headed into the great unknown, into a life so different from anything Marian had ever experienced and in truth, she was a little terrified.

Robin shifted beside her, breaking an apple down the middle and handing over half.

"You gonna be alright?" Robin took a bite of the apple.

Marian pursed her lips and looked down at her half. She would likely never eat another gourmet meal again and while the gold that they took from the treasury was more substantial than anything she'd ever held in her hands at once before - it was still only enough to purchase a modest living.

Marian had very little memory of what it had been like to live on the street - mostly just disjointed images of the dark and feelings of bone-chilling cold. So, a majority of her memories involved being surrounded by luxury - fancy meals, luxurious clothes, and handmaidens waiting on her hand and foot. Despite all of this, however, Marian still found herself happier than she could remember having been in a long time, sitting on this hill, covered in dust from the road, with Robin.

Marian wasn't afraid of this new life she'd chosen, only the unknown and now she would never have to face anything alone again. With a smile, Marian turned to face Robin, taking her free hand in hers and intertwining their fingers.

"Yeah." Marian squeezed Robin's hand. "I am."

Chapter Nine

Marian woke, surrounded by warmth - Robin's arms wrapped around her bare waist. She hummed happily, scooting back into her lover's embrace as Robin lifted a hand to her breast and gently ran her thumb over her pebbling nipple. Marian tilted her chin, exposing her neck as Robin leaned forward, pressing light kisses to her pulse point, feeling her heartbeat speeding up in excitement.

"Again?" Marian teased, pressing her ass up against Robin's lap and reaching back to grip her lover's thigh. "Even after last night?"

"Mmm." Robin began kissing her neck more deeply, allowing her tongue to dart out, following a series of love bites. "Can you really blame me? We spent years not being able to wake up in each other's arms - forgive me if I'm a little... impatient to get my hands on you."

Marian smiled, turning over onto her back and pulling Robin on top of her, running her hands up and down the curve of Robin's waist sensually.

"There is nothing to forgive, unless of course, you plan on

working me up and not finishing me off - in which case you might actually need to beg for forgiveness."

Robin smiled, her red hair tumbling enticingly over her naked shoulder.

"I would never." Robin pushed herself up, gripping Marian's thighs and straddling one, pressing her own thigh up against Marian's core.

Marian gasped, her hands shifting automatically to Robin's hips as her lover began moving, creating a delicious friction between her legs. Unwilling to go another moment without kissing her, Marian tangled her fingers in Robin's wild hair, pulling their lips together for a messy kiss. She moaned deeply as Robin rolled her hips, feeling her lover get wetter as she pulled back with a gasp.

"I need..." Marian whimpered, squirming under Robin's touch. Robin leaned back in, connecting their lips once more as she reoriented them into exactly the position Marian had been asking for, leaning back and moving her hips forward, slotting their legs.

Marian moaned loudly as she felt their pussies grind together, Robin continued to move her hips, now watching her pleasured faces from a distance. Marian could feel her arousal building as she encouraged Robin's hips the best she could.

"Fuck, baby..." Robin cursed. "You're so wet. You're gonna make me cum."

Marian could only gasp and fight to keep her eyes open. As much as the pleasure demanded that she screw her eyes shut, she wasn't about to miss the ecstasy on Robin's face as she teetered over the edge. She could tell that Robin was close by the way she panted, hips stuttering as she continued to grind. The friction mixed with the torrent of moans and whimpers spilling from her lover's lips sent Marian hurtling towards orgasm faster than anything else could and before she knew it, she was riding that edge right there with Robin.

"Oh shit." Robin whimpered. "Here it comes... fuck... Marian-"

Marian felt Robin's pussy twitch as she came, pushing her over as well. Marian gasped, pressing her hips back up into Robin to work them through it - crying out as their clits brushed, sending another fiery rush through her body as a second wave of her climax hit. They continued like that, suspended in mutual pleasure for what felt like an eternity as Marian felt her whole body seize up.

Then, finally after the pleasure had peaked, Robin fell forward, connecting their lips and continuing a slow grind to work through the aftershocks.

Marian panted to catch her breath, her lips traveling from Robin's, down her lover's jaw, neck, and to her shoulder where she finally hooked her chin, wrapping her arms around the redhead's waist.

"What a wonderful start to my day." Marian hummed in amusement, eliciting a quiet chuckle from Robin.

"If only we could stay in bed all day." Robin mused, sitting up, letting the sheets fall to the wayside and giving Marian a view of her stark nakedness. Marian grinned, stretching her arms above her head with a yawn before turning to her side seductively.

"If only." Marian teased, watching as Robin took in her curves, biting at her bottom lip. "But alas, I have a garden to tend and you have a Willa to meet."

"Mmm, unfortunate." Robin grinned, leaning down and

pressing a quick kiss to Marian's lips before sitting up and hopping out of bed.

They'd been officially gone for three months now, settling into a cottage just outside a nice, little coastal town. It was everything Marian had hoped it would be - her garden was filled with vegetables and herbs that would be ready to sell by the end of the season, they were only a five minute walk from the beach, and they'd even adopted a stray cat who happened to show up to their cottage before they did.

Of course Marian knew that Robin missed the Merry Men, but luckily, they'd managed to stay in touch and Robin, unable to stay out of trouble for long, had been ecstatic about Willa's most recent letter asking for her assistance in planning a hit.

Marian reclined in bed for a little while longer, watching as Robin got dressed and happily accepting another kiss before Robin grabbed her bag, heading for the door.

After Robin left for town, Marian put on her gardening pants and apron and made her way out front. Picking up her pruning shears and spade, Marian settled on the ground next to her cucumber plants, taking in the warmth of the sun interspersed with refreshing ocean breezes as she pinned up her hair and got to work.

She was practically shoulder deep in dirt when the sound of approaching horse hooves caused her to look up.

"Maid Marian?" A gentleman on a horse with a shoulder bag filled with letters came trotting over, stopping right outside her gate.

"Yes?" Marian stood, brushing the dirt from her hands onto her apron.

"Letter for you, mum." The man reached into his satchel and pulled out a single letter, presenting it to Marian.

"Thank you." Marian smiled, taking the letter and before she could say anything else, the man turned his horse around and took off further down the coast.

Marian watched him leave and looked down at the letter, front and back, unable to find any indication of whom it was from, only "Maid Marian" written on the front in elegant script.

As she opened the letter, Marian sat atop her garden's stone wall, looking out over the ocean. Inside was a single piece of paper along with two newspaper clippings, but before she even looked to see what they said, Marian sat for a moment, in shock, holding the paper.

The only thing written on it was a single letter, but even so, it was written in a script that she knew almost as well as she knew her own writing.

There in the center of the paper was the letter, J.

Tucking the paper back into the envelope, Marian hurriedly looked down to the clippings. The first seemed to be an addendum to an obituary. It read:

Philip Mark, Sheriff of Nottingham for over two decades passed in a robbery several months ago. The initial obituary that was run in this bulletin had several marked mistakes printed that now require retraction after further investigation.

The late Sheriff will no longer retain his badge of honor in service to the Crown after an investigation revealed extreme levels of embezzlement on the part of Mark.

The investigation into his death, still considered a murder, has been formally closed by the Crown in light of the embezzlement charges.

Marian blinked several times in surprise, even needing to re-read the clipping before it truly sunk in - this meant that nobody was going to be coming after them. Despite knowing that John hadn't sent anyone their way in the past three months, it was a different level of relief knowing that it was actually over. There was no need for them to keep looking over their shoulder, or waiting for the other shoe to drop. Despite everything, John was still looking out for her.

Taking a shaky breath, Marian slipped the first clipping back into the envelope and looked down at the second. It was an announcement.

An engagement is announced between Prince John of Nottingham and Duchess Inta of Mansfield. The nuptials, to be conducted in four months from this date, will serve to form a lasting alliance between Nottingham and Mansfield, further bolstering the stability of the region under King Henry II.

Marian couldn't help but smile to herself as she ran her finger over the paper. He really did know her so well; in one fell swoop, John had eased her fears and reassured her that he was alright without even penning a single word.

Looking out at the horizon on the sparkling water, Marian sighed, taking in the salty ocean air. Perhaps she would ask Robin if they could go back to Nottingham for the wedding. Grinning to herself, Marian placed the last newspaper clipping back in the envelope before hopping off the wall and heading back inside.

As she made her lunch, settling down at her table with a cup of tea, Marian relaxed, finally feeling completely at peace.

Acknowledgments

To Aly Hollis and Tereza Kane - thank you for going on this crazy journey with me, I am excited about everything coming next!

To my husband - thank you for coming to every single event with me and always supporting my dreams. You mean everything to me.

To my parents - thank you for always being my biggest fans, I truly couldn't ask for better parents.

About the Author

Harlowe Savage is a queer author dedicated to creating stories that depict queer romances with the same amount of spice and passion that readers get from their straight counterparts. She firmly believes that the gap between the amount of LGBTQIA+ erotica and heterosexual erotica in the mainstream is far too large and intends to rectify this through normalizing queer romance novels and increasing accessibility of the genre.

Flipped Fairytales

Rob Me Blindly Halowe Savage

Wish Me Freely Aly Hollis

Drown Me Gently Tereza Kane